Chugga-chugga

choo-choo

Kevin Lewis

Pictures by Daniel Kirk

HYPERION BOOKS FOR CHILDREN · NEW YORK

Sun's up!
Morning's here.
Up and at 'em,
engineer.

Chugga-chugga
choo-choo,
whistle blowing,

Hurry! Hurry!
Load the
freight.
To the city.
Can't be late.

Through the country
on the loose.
Engine black
and red caboose.

Chugga-chugga choo-choo,

wheels a-turning,

whoooooOoo!

whOoooooOooo!

'Round the mountains, high and steep.
Through the valleys, low and deep.

Into tunnels, underground.
See the darkness. Hear the sound.
Chugga-chugga choo-choo, echo calling,

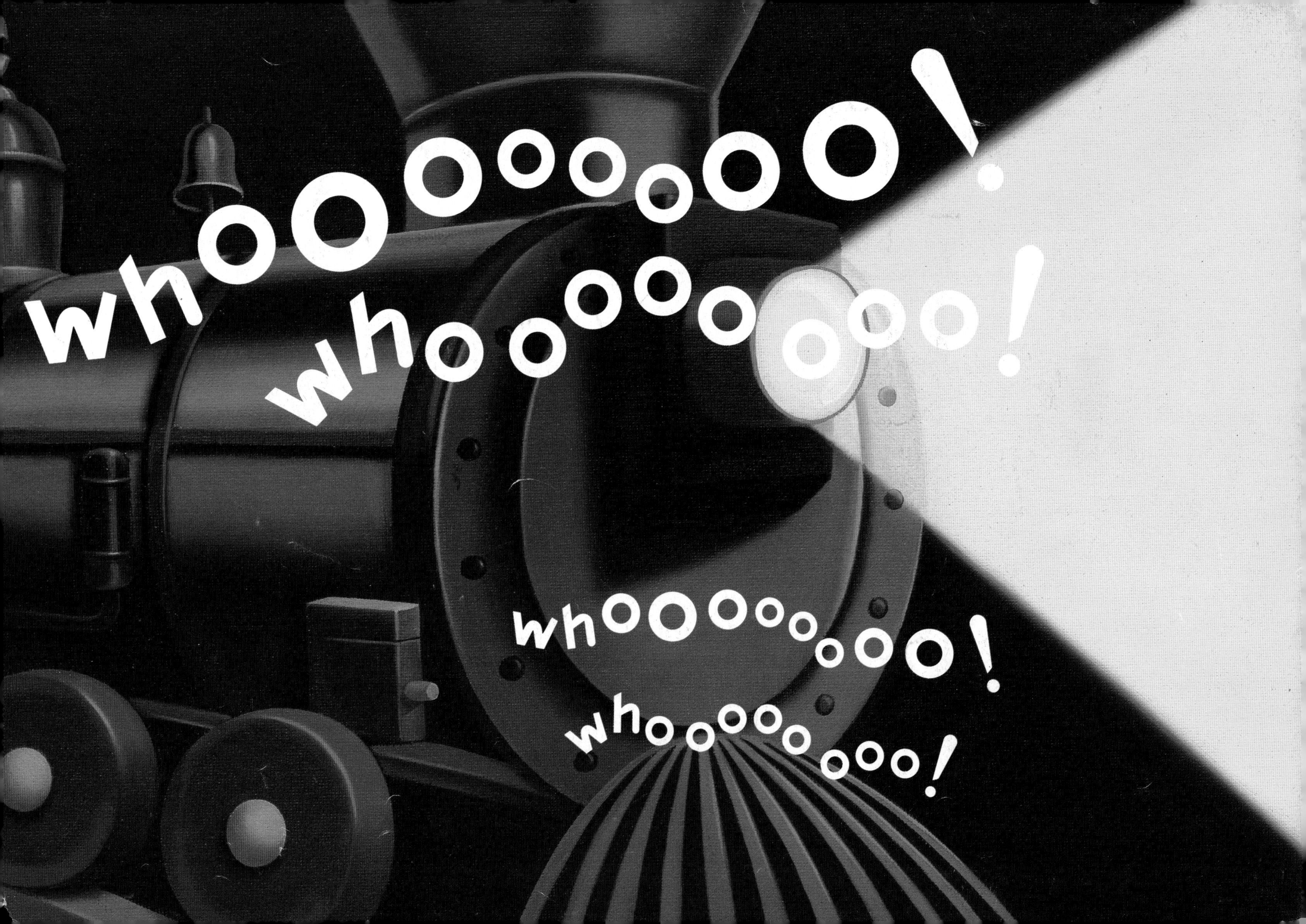
whooooooooo!
whooooooooo!
whooooooooo!
whoooooooo!

Across the river, swift and wide.

A bridge goes to the other side.

Chugga-chugga choo-choo, there's the city,

In the station workers wait,
ready to unload the freight.

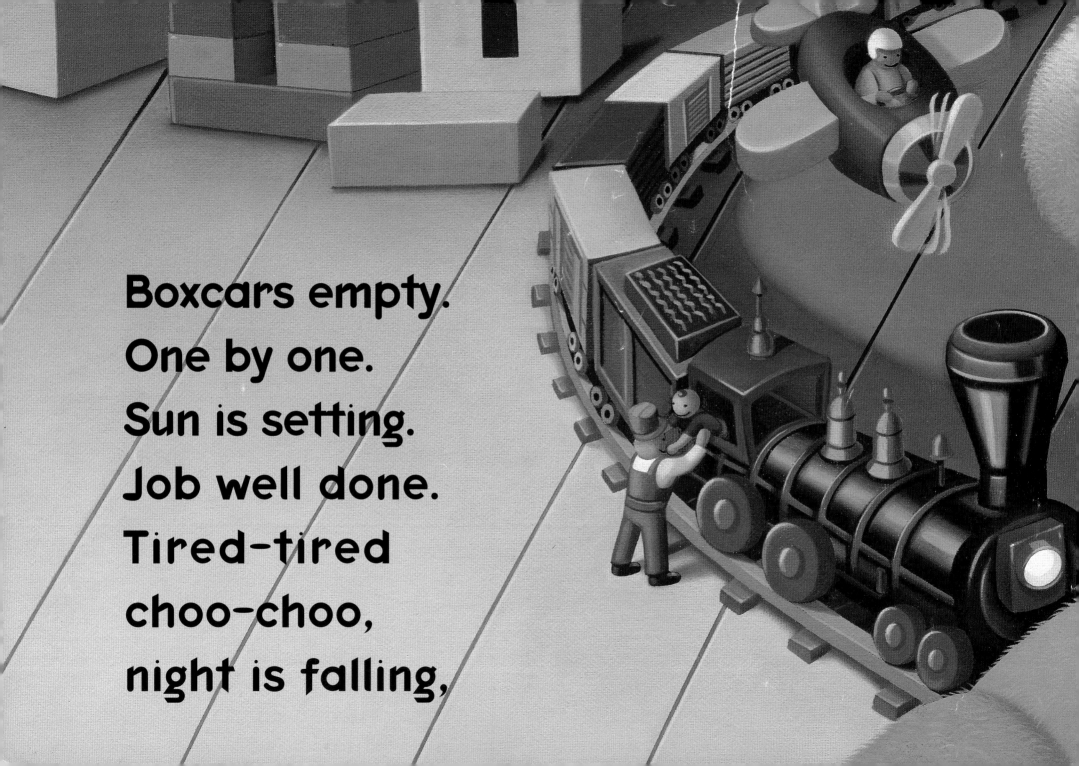

Boxcars empty.
One by one.
Sun is setting.
Job well done.
Tired-tired
choo-choo,
night is falling,

To the roundhouse
you are bound.
Good night, engine,
safe and sound.

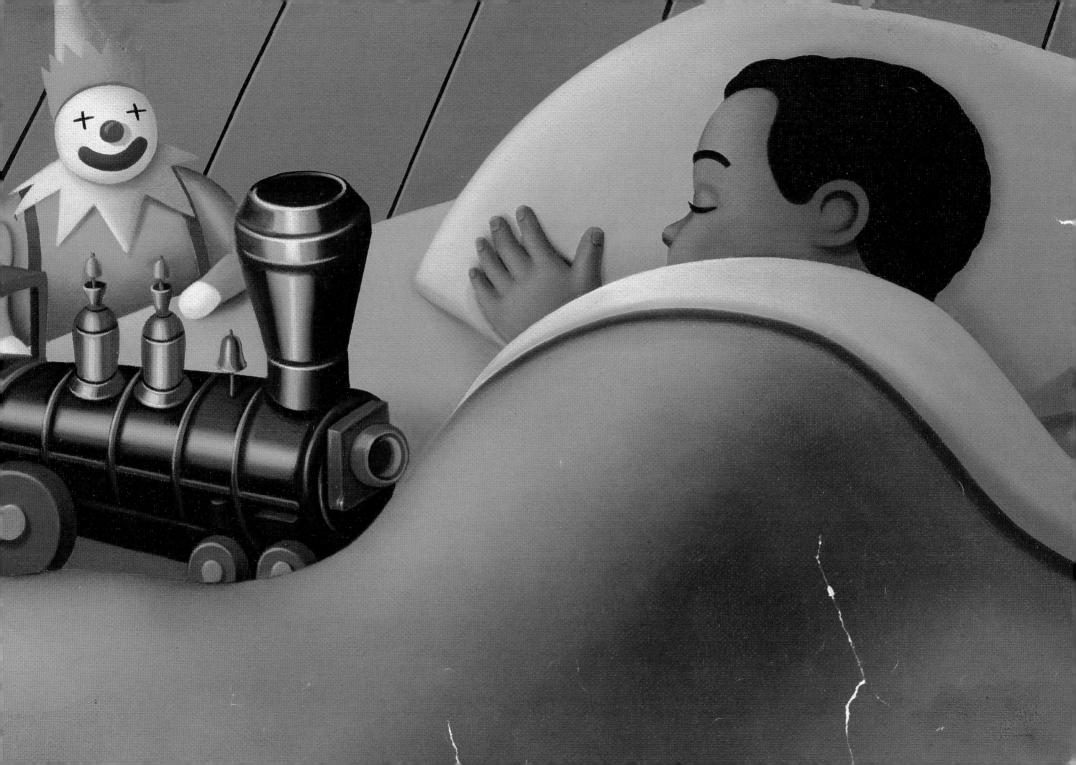

Sleepy-sleepy choo-choo,
till tomorrow,

whoooooooo
whoooooo

and Zan,
keep on chuggin'.
—K. L.

For Russell,
the little conductor with the great big toot.
—D. K.

Text © 1999 by Kevin Lewis
Illustrations © 1999 by Daniel Kirk

For information address
Disney • HYPERION,
125 West End Avenue, New York,
New York, 10023.

Printed in Malaysia

First Hardcover Edition, May 1999

17 19 20 18   H106-9333-5-15115

Library of Congress Cataloging-in-Publication Data
Lewis, Kevin.
Chugga-chugga choo-choo/ by Kevin Lewis; illustrated by Daniel
Kirk.—1st ed.
p.   cm.
Summary: A rhyming story about a freight train's day, from load-
ing freight in the morning to retiring to the roundhouse after the
day's work is done.
ISBN 0-7868-0429-7 (trade)—ISBN 0-7868-2379-8 (lib. bdg.)
[1. Railroads—trains—Fiction. 2. Stories in rhyme.] I. Kirk,
Daniel, ill. II. Title.
PZ8.3L5857Ch   1998
[E]—dc21   98-42101